The Emperor's New Clothes

Illustrated by Jack and Irene Delano

The Emperor's New Clothes

Illustrated by Jack and Irene Delano

WITH TEXT ADAPTED FROM HANS CHRISTIAN ANDERSEN AND OTHER SOURCES
BY JEAN VAN LEEUWEN

RANDOM HOUSE 🏠 NEW YORK

NOV 8 1972

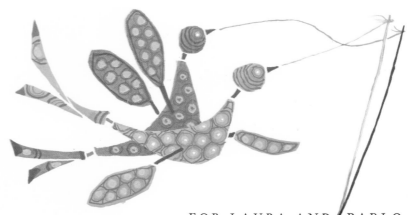

FOR LAURA AND PABLO

Many years ago in a faraway kingdom there lived an emperor who was excessively fond of clothes. He had almost no time at all for ruling his country. He much preferred to parade down the streets, showing off his newest robes.

Once every hour he changed his clothes, and he had so many that he almost never wore the same suit more than once a year. He could scarcely ever be found in his court. Instead his courtiers always said, "The emperor is in his dressing room."

The capital of the kingdom was a gay and lively city, full of visitors from far-off places. One day two strangers arrived, claiming to be master weavers. They were taken at once to the emperor.

"Our cloth is unequaled in all the world," they told the emperor. "Not only is it more beautiful, softer, and lighter than any other but it has magical powers as well. This cloth is invisible to anyone who is a fool. Think about it, Your Majesty!"

So the emperor thought, and he decided he would like very much to have some of this unusual cloth. "I shall have it made into a suit," he said. "Then I will know that whoever does not admire my magical suit is a fool and unfit for his position. In this way, I shall be able to rid my court of fools!"

He paid the weavers a large sum of money and
ordered them to begin work at once.

The weavers set up their loom and demanded quan-
tities of thread spun from the purest silk and gold and silver. Secretly they put all of this into their trunks. Then,
without an inch of thread on their loom, they went through
the motions of weaving. These were not master weavers.
They were not weavers at all. They were swindlers!

News of the magical cloth spread swiftly through the city. All of the people began looking at each other, wondering which of them was a fool. And everyone worried secretly that he might not be able to see the cloth himself.

After a few days, the emperor thought he would like to see how the cloth was coming along. But he hesitated. Would he be able to see it? Was it possible that he might be a fool? "Certainly not," he said to himself. "Still, I think I will send one of my advisers first."

He chose his prime minister, the wisest man in the kingdom.

So the prime minister went to the place where the two weavers were busily pretending to weave. When he saw the empty loom, the old man's eyes opened wide. "Why, I cannot see a thing!" he thought. But he took care not to say so.

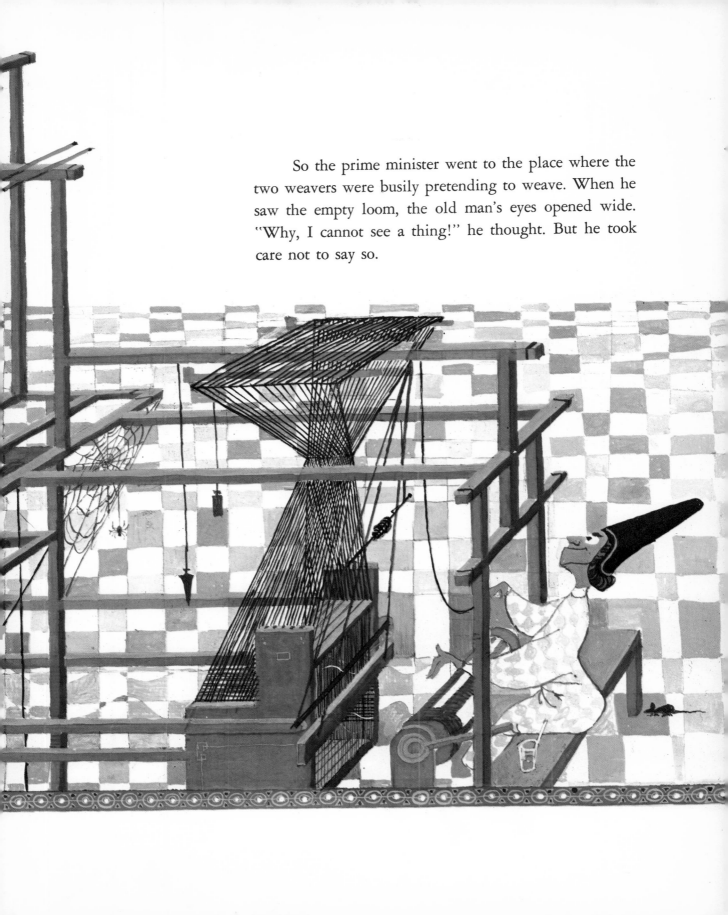

"Pray, step a little closer, Your Excellency," said the weavers. "Have you ever seen such an exquisite design? Are not the colors brilliant?"

The prime minister stared as hard as he could, but he could see nothing at all. For of course there was nothing to see. "Is it possible," thought he, "that I am a fool? If that is so, no one must know."

"Beautiful! Simply beautiful!" he said quickly. "I

will certainly tell the emperor that I am greatly pleased."

"We are delighted that you approve," said the weavers. They proceeded to describe the color and design of the imaginary cloth. "See the richness of the gold border," they said. "And the delicacy of the leaf pattern on the sleeves. His Majesty will be delighted." The prime minister carefully memorized every detail and went off to tell the emperor.

As the days went by, the weavers demanded more money and more gold and silver and silk thread. The emperor gave them everything they asked for, and they put it all into their trunks. But the loom remained as bare as before.

Just to be on the safe side, the emperor decided to send one more official to see the cloth before looking at it himself. The imperial general stood dumbfounded before the empty loom. Try as he might he could not see the tiniest bit of cloth. "It is a trick," he told himself. But he remembered that the prime minister had been able to see the cloth. "That is strange," he thought. "If

he saw it, why can't I? Is he a wise man and am I a fool?
If that is so, no one must know."

"Magnificent!" he said in a loud voice.

"We were sure you would like it," said the weavers.
They pointed out the rich colors and the intricate designs.
And the imperial general listened closely and went off
to tell the emperor.

Excitement was growing in the city. The people talked of nothing but the marvelous new cloth which the weavers were making for the emperor.

At last the emperor decided to look at the cloth for himself. Accompanied by the prime minister, and the imperial general, and the most important nobles of his court, he went to visit the weavers.

But when he stood in front of the empty loom his heart sank, for of course he could see nothing at all.

The prime minister and the imperial general admired the cloth excitedly. "Just look at the gold border, Your Majesty," they said. "How elegant it is! And the leaf design on the sleeves—how stylish!" And they kept pointing at the loom, for each thought the other could see the cloth.

"How is it possible," thought the emperor, "that what they see so clearly I cannot see at all? Are they wise men? Am I a fool? No, it cannot be. But if it is so, no one must know."

"Never in my life have I seen such perfection!" he exclaimed. "I shall wear a suit of this cloth in the grand procession next week."

The emperor ordered the weavers to have his new clothes ready in a week's time. And for the extraordinary work they had done, he made each of them a Knight of the Realm.

The weavers now pretended to work harder than ever. Late into every night they kept their candles lit so the townspeople might see how busy they were. They went through the motions of taking cloth off the loom.

They cut and snipped and stitched and sewed. But their scissors cut only air, and they sewed with needles that had no thread. At last they announced, "The emperor's new clothes are ready."

Accompanied by his nobles, the emperor again paid the weavers a visit. The two swindlers raised their arms high as if holding something. "Here are the trousers, Your Majesty," they said. "And this is the cloak. And just look at the mantle and the stockings and the train! The entire suit is no heavier than a spider's web. When you wear it you will almost think you have nothing on at all. But that is the beauty of it, is it not?"

"Oh, yes, yes indeed!" said all the nobles, though of course they could see no trousers or cloak or anything at all.

"If Your Majesty will be good enough to undress,"
said the weavers, "you may try on the suit without delay."

So the emperor took off all his clothes, and the
weavers pretended to fit the new suit to him. They pulled

it down a little here. They adjusted it there. "How does
it feel around the waist?" they asked. "Is it at all too
tight? Are the sleeves too long?"

"Oh no," said the emperor. "It fits perfectly."

He turned around and around in front of the mirror. "How do I look?" he asked.

"Marvelous!" cried all the nobles in unison. "How becoming the clothes are! The gold border! That delicate leaf design!"

"Then let the grand procession begin!" commanded the emperor.

So the royal chamberlains bent down and pretended to lift the emperor's train. With hands held high, they carefully carried the train that was not there.

Outside crowds of people had been gathering all day to see the emperor's new clothes. Everyone was curious. Everyone was there.

The trumpets sounded and the emperor marched proudly forth. "Oh, how splendid he looks in his new clothes!" the people cried. "How perfectly they fit! What a magnificent train!" No one would admit to seeing no clothes at all, for no one wanted to be thought a fool. The royal chamberlains even began to feel as if they were carrying a real train after all.

Suddenly a child's voice rang out...

Through the crowd a whisper spread. "Did you hear what the child said? He's naked! The emperor has nothing on!"

The whisper quickly grew to a roar. "Nothing on! Nothing on! The emperor has nothing on!" cried the people.

And the emperor trembled, for he knew it was true.

But the trumpets went on blaring and the cymbals went on clashing, so what could the emperor do except go marching straight ahead? And the royal chamberlains held up the invisible train as high as if it had been real.

THE END

About the story

The story of the clever swindlers and the foolish king existed long before Hans Christian Andersen wrote down the tale he called *The Emperor's New Clothes* in about 1835.

More than six hundred years ago a Spanish writer, Don Juan Manuel, included a similar story in his collection of tales, *El Conde Lucanor.* In his version the one who finally dared to tell the truth was a black servant who said to the king, "My Lord, I am a poor man and have nothing to lose. Therefore I say to you, either I am blind or you are going about naked."

Three hundred years later the famous writer Miguel de Cervantes used this story as the basis for a comic play that delighted audiences in all the theaters of Spain. But the tale in *El Conde Lucanor* is the earliest written version we know about. Its Moorish setting suggests that Don Juan may have heard it from a Moorish storyteller. But where did the Moor first hear the story? Probably it was passed down to him through generations of storytellers.

In Ceylon, an island off the coast of India, an ancient folktale tells of a king who was tricked into riding naked about the streets on the back of an elephant. Did this tale come from the East to Spain along the Arab trade routes? Or did it travel in the opposite direction? All we know is that the story of the emperor will last forever because in every man's heart is the hope that there will always be someone to speak the truth where there is hypocrisy. And because as long as there are foolish grownups in the world, there will be children who cannot be fooled.

The text in this book is based on the story as Andersen told it. But in their illustrations the artists have drawn from all of the sources above to show that this is a tale for all time and for all people.